MOLLY BANG

One Fall Day

Greenwillow Books, New York

The full-color art, collage constructions, was photographed by Tom Kleindinst
to retain the three-dimensional quality of the originals.
The text type is Kabel Demi.
In the illustration on page 6, the painting on the wall is by Hui-ming Wang.

Printed in Singapore by Tien Wah Press
First Edition   10   9   8   7   6   5   4   3   2   1

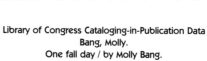

Library of Congress Cataloging-in-Publication Data
Bang, Molly.
One fall day / by Molly Bang.
p.   cm.
Summary: At bedtime, a sleepy child listens as her mother
describes the events of the day, which are illustrated in three-dimensional
pictures featuring the child's favorite toys.
ISBN 0-688-07015-9 (trade).   ISBN 0-688-07016-7 (lib. bdg.)
[1. Bedtime—Fiction.   2. Play—Fiction.
3. Toys—Fiction.   4. Afro-Americans—Fiction.]   I. Title.
PZ7.B2217On   1994   [E]—dc20
93-36490   CIP   AC

To Old Sunshine
Monika

and
to her young
grandmother
Betsy

With many thanks to Ivette, Joan, Judy,

Mary Lou, Penny, and Rayna for cutting leaves

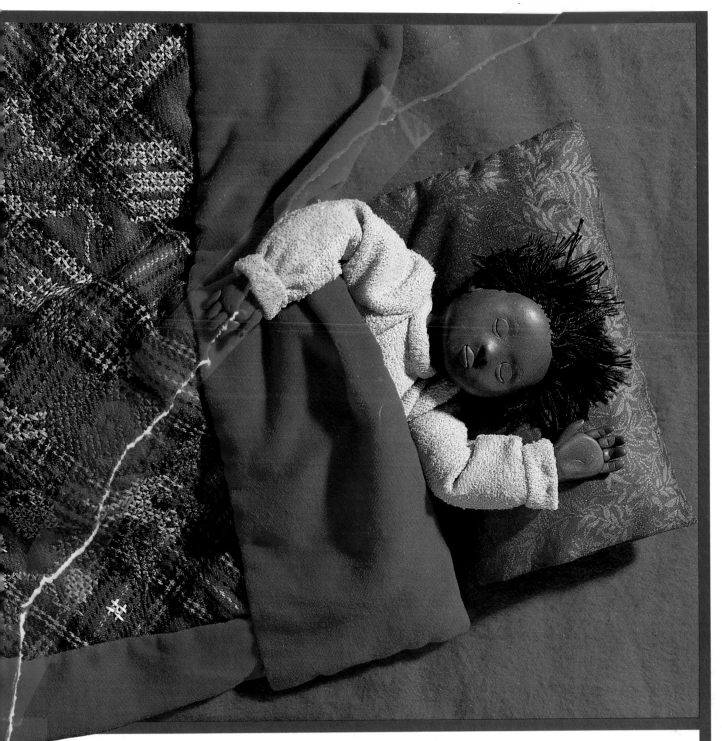

When you sleep, gray cat curls close
and watches over you all night.
Sleep now, sleep beneath your warm, red quilt.

In the morning, when you wake,
your friends wake with you.

Gray cat stretches, polar bear blinks,
dinosaur sniffs, paper crane flutters, yellow ball rolls,
and car waits on the floor.

Your friends eat with you—juice from golden oranges, corn muffins and butter, eggs from clucking chickens, and milk from Jersey cows.

Yellow ball rolls, and car waits on the floor.
Crane watches yellow leaves fall outside the door.

You play with your friends under the yellow leaves.

You catch and throw, you sing and swing,
you hide and slide and ride.

You listen.

You hear the truck go *rmmm rmmm*.

You hear the train go *chugga chugga TOOT TOOT*.

You hear the marsh reeds whisper in the wind.
Can you hear the waves crash on the beach?
Can you hear the thunder rumble in the clouds?

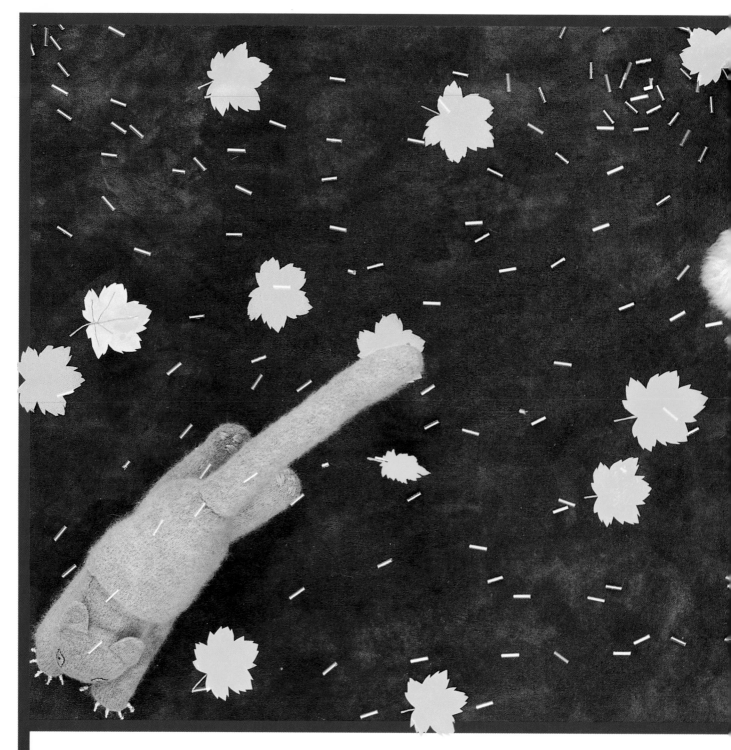

Rain beats down on you.
Wind swirls the rain in circles, sweeps it sideways,
lifts you up to fly like yellow leaves.

Gray cat digs her claws into the grass and clings.

The storm has passed.
Polar bear holds you. You hold cat and yellow ball.
Crane holds out her paper wings to dry.

Dinosaur sees that you are safe, and car waits on the grass.
Round drops of rain shine in your black hair
and on the scattered yellow leaves.

What do you do in the afternoon?
You rake, you pull, you dig, you carry,
you hug, you read, you paint.

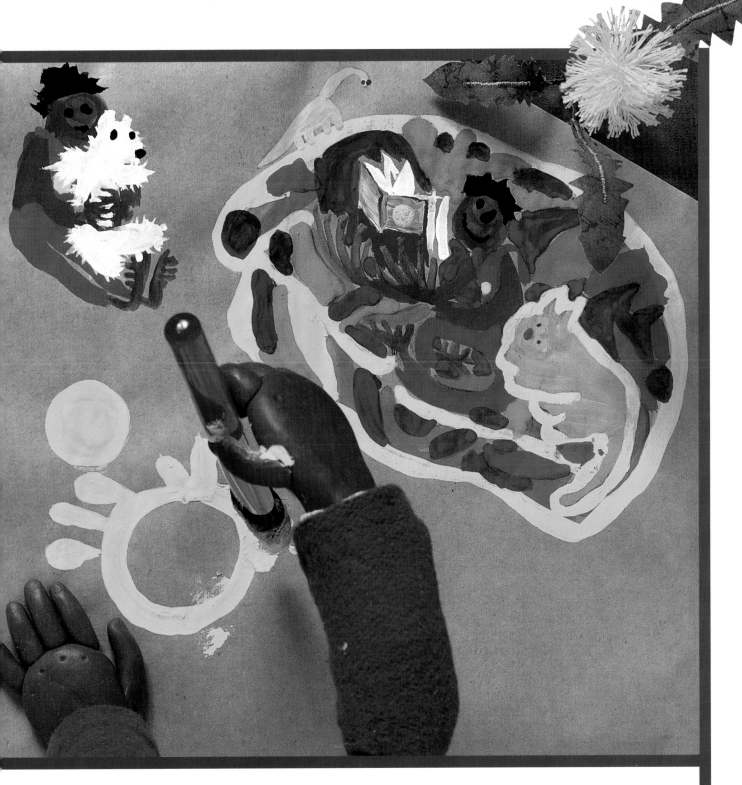

And when you paint with yellow,
what are the yellow things you make?

The sun sinks down behind the trees
and casts long shadows on the grass.
You come inside.

Slowly, slowly, slowly you pull car.
Cat follows bear, and dinosaur rolls ball.
Crane waits on the roof until you all come home.

After supper, you've had your bath,
you've brushed your teeth,
you're snuggled warm in bed.

What now?

Now you close your eyes and sleep.
Gray cat curls close and watches over you all night.
You and your friends will play again tomorrow.